My Special Day
at Third Street School

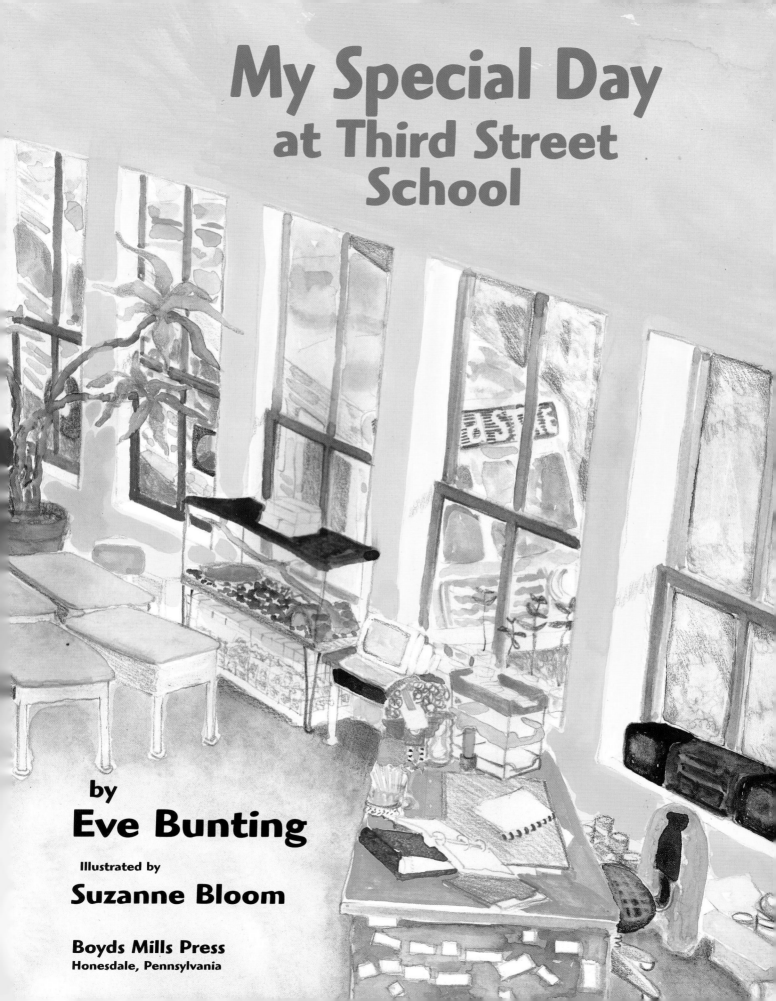

My Special Day
at Third Street School

by
Eve Bunting

Illustrated by
Suzanne Bloom

Boyds Mills Press
Honesdale, Pennsylvania

For Caroline and Herma, with love
—E. B.

To teachers and teaching artists, still in awe of their calling.
Thanks to them and to E.B. for sharing a world of possibilities.
Thanks to Fred for seeing to the details
—S. B.

Text copyright © 2004 by Eve Bunting
Illustrations copyright © 2004 by Suzanne Bloom

Boyds Mills Press, Inc.
815 Church Street
Honesdale, Pennsylvania 18431
Printed in China

The Library of Congress has cataloged the hardcover edition
of this book as follows:

Library of Congress Cataloging-in-Publication Data

Bunting, Eve.
    My special day at Third Street School / by Eve Bunting ;
illustrated by Suzanne Bloom. —1st ed.
[32] p. : col. ill. ;   cm.
Summary: A school visit from children's book author Amanda Drake
brings a day full of fun.
ISBN 978-1-59078-075-6 (hc.)
ISBN 978-1-59078-745-8 (pbk.)
1. Schools—Fiction. 2. Authors—Fiction.
I. Bloom, Suzanne, ill. II. Title.
   [E] 21 PZ7.B868My 2004
2003108157

First edition
First paperback edition, 2009
The text of this book is set in 15-point Stone Serif.
The illustrations are done in gouache, colored pencil, and crayon.

(hc.) 10 9 8 7 6
(pbk.) 10 9 8 7 6 5 4 3 2 1

AN AUTHOR'S COMING TO OUR SCHOOL.
Our teacher's so excited.
The author wrote and said that she
was glad to be invited.

Her name is Miss Amanda Drake.
She's coming on the bus
from over on Biloxi Street
just to visit us.

First, of course, we read her books . . .
every one we've got.
Then we borrow fourteen more.
She's written quite a lot.

We make a welcome banner
that we hang up in the hall.
We draw a million drawings
just to decorate the wall.

We fold some origami flowers.
They're very hard to do.
We pile them in a basket
with a note that says "For You."

We make a list of questions
that we'll ask Amanda Drake.
Our teacher says "Don't ask her,
'How much money do you make?'"

We squeeze some ice-cold lemonade.
We bake a chocolate cake.
Our classroom's looking beautiful
for Miss Amanda Drake.

She's here! She's here! We're in a state
of great anticipation!
We stamp our feet and clap our hands
to show appreciation.

Amanda Drake is tall and thin.
Her hair is streaked with pink.
It doesn't sound attractive,
but it's nicer than you think.

She talks to us and reads to us
and says she loves to write.
"I'm working, working every day
and sometimes every night.

"Verbs and nouns and adjectives,
words that show and tell.
My dictionary's close at hand
for words that I can't spell.

"There's something that I'd like to share
because it's truly true.
It doesn't seem like work
if you are loving what you do."

She cuddles all our animals.
She asks to hold our snake.
She says she has a rat at home.
I LOVE Amanda Drake!

I'm nervous, but I raise my hand.
"It would be really cool
if you would write a book about
your visit to our school."

"My goodness! What a great idea!
When I go home, I'll try it.
If I can do a super job,
a publisher may buy it."

I'm feeling really clever now.
I bounce around my seat.

I *whomp* my glass of lemonade.
It splashes on my feet.

The ice cubes slide like pebbles
that you skim across the sea.
Amanda Drake gives one a kick,
and then she winks at me!

I should have been embarrassed,
but I'm not. In fact I think
I must be extra special
to be favored with a wink.

We wave good-bye as she climbs
on the intercity bus.

She leans out of the window
and waves right back at us.

We're writing lots of stories.
We're writing more and more.

Amanda Drake inspired us . . .
In fact, I've written four!

In honor of our author,
we have now renamed our snake.
Instead of Sally Sunshine,
she is now Amanda Drake.

Last week we got a letter.
She says her day was great.
She says she's working on our book.
It's very hard to wait!

At last, at last the book is done.
We love the dedication:
To all the kids at Third Street School
with love and admiration.

We hope *you* like it just as much.
We hope that it's a hit.
It's called *My Special Day at Third Street School.*
And guess what?

THIS IS IT.